# Hitomi's Path

a story of another Japan

by

M. L. Buchman

Buchman Bookworks

Copyright 2014 Matthew Lieber Buchman
Published by Buchman Bookworks
All rights reserved.
This book, or parts thereof,
may not be reproduced in any form
without permission from the author.
Discover more by this author at:
www.mlbuchman.com
Cover image:
Dangerous Asian Girl
© Igor Kovalchuk | Dreamstime.com

# Other works by M.L. Buchman

<u>Science Fiction & Fantasy</u>
*Nara*
*Monk's Maze*

Dieties Anonymous
*Cookbook from Hell: Reheated*
*Saviors 101*

<u>Thrillers</u>
*Swap Out!*
*One Chef*

<u>Romances</u>
The Night Stalkers
*The Night Is Mine*
*I Own the Dawn*
*Daniel's Christmas*
*Wait Until Dark*
*Frank's Independence Day*
*Peter's Christmas*
*Take Over at Midnight*
*Light Up the Night*

Firehawks
*Pure Heat*
*Wildfire at Dawn*
*Full Blaze*

Angelo's Hearth
*Where Dreams are Born*
*Where Dreams Reside*
*Maria's Christmas Table*
*Where Dreams Unfold*
*Where Dreams Are Written*

1

**"You must lock this** memory away from your own sight."

Hitomi Yamada of the *Mura* clan knelt before the single *tatami* mat in the center of the vast training-temple courtyard beneath a blue sky. A hundred pairs of warriors could spar here without interfering with one another, as she had countless times. But now, there was only herself kneeling in the sand, her clan's master, and an aged bluebird who had chosen to live its days in the courtyard. The vast expanse echoed with the silent energy of those many fighters, held within the temple's out-stretched arms of dark cypress wood walls.

She knew that Master Tanka spoke truth, though Hitomi didn't like to block pieces of her mind. But a *Mura* knew the warrior's discipline better than any mere soldier of Japan. As with each of the clans of Japan in the five centuries since their country had been masked from the rest of the world, she was bred to her role, then trained from birth. The *Mura* were the dark fighters born to stealth and single combat. Her nervous system was faster, her patience greater, and her silences deeper.

Even now at seventeen, it had been three years since she'd first dealt death in the night behind guarded walls, yet made it appear as if the target had died in their sleep.

Now Master Tanka, the leader of the stealth warriors, ordered that she block a piece of her memory. With careful focus Hitomi sealed it where none, but one, could ever learn what she no longer knew.

# 2

***Hitomi dropped to her*** knees before the Shinto shrine a week's journey from the temple of the *Mura* to rest and to consider her dilemma. It was a nice shrine. The structure stood just the height of a woman, five *shaku* tall. A comfortable height, allowing Hitomi to rest on the trail passing by the *kami's* feet and look up to its face without straining.

The red-and-white paint on his scowling features was kept fresh by the local Buddhists who sought harmony with the whimsical Shinto spirits. The small shrine was clean, but in this remote location it had few offerings about its feet, a small bag of rice, a few coins. That was all that lay on the small step and she had scant more to add.

Hitomi bowed until her forehead touched the earth and remained so until her breathing settled. Perhaps the spirit of the shrine would help her. Hitomi had crossed many *ri* these last days and had many more to travel before her journey would be complete. Returning to a kneeling position, she had to pull the *katana* killing sword and its sheath from her back to sit upon her heels.

Japan had remained untouched in all of the years since the Great Massacre that had vanquished the foreigners who called themselves Portuguese. The founders of the *Mura* clan had made sure that not a single one of the round-eyed devils had returned to their ships to take word of the Japans out into the unwanted world.

Twice since, the Chinese emperor had sent fleets of tall-masted ships and twice they had been defeated. Once by a mighty typhoon sent by the gods, may their years be blessed. And once by the great master Tiyama of the *Musou*, deceiving the chief steersman of the Chinese fleet in his dreams and leading their emperor's entire fleet onto the rocky cliffs of Kyushu, may their sharp rocks and the fast swords of the *Mura* clan be blessed.

None had come since.

The *Musou* clan, the dreamers of Japan, had cast a dream-mask around the islands. It was whispered that Tiyama had spent all the power of the greatest mystic of the dreamer clan, Jun, to achieve this miracle. Ever since, the great land of Nippon showed on no maps, existed in no one's memory beyond the mask, nor could the islands be seen from water or sky.

A ship of the outside could enter from the east and sail out the west and never know they had crossed the heart of the world. They were now truly the Floating Kingdom.

But the message Hitomi bore in her sworn-and-sealed memory struck at the balance of that heart. She remembered that much and no more. Not until she looked upon the face of the Japanese Emperor would the memory be released that had been locked away—the face of the Son of Heaven had been the key she had placed upon her own mind. Master Tanka had agreed that only the Son of Heaven, enthroned in far off Edo, would know what to do.

The message was too important to trust to the walkers of the *Musou* clan. They traveled the country in great year-long circuits to maintain the dream. They were also the carriers of words. But this news could not take the risk of a year's time to reach its destination.

Nor the risk of it failing to arrive.

At the temple gate Master Tanka had stopped her and called her, "Child of my eye." Hitomi's name meant, "she of the pretty eyes," but he spoke to her as a father to a child grown.

"This is a burden you shall carry. For it must move faster than the wind, lighter than the hawk, and above all, it must reach the Emperor."

According to the records, Hitomi, at seventeen summers old, was the youngest *kunoichi,* the youngest female *ninja* in the five-century history of the *Mura* clan. So she knew she must struggle twice as hard to be wise.

She bowed again over her sword, praying to the shrine's *kami* for guidance. If it heard, it didn't answer. She'd never heard the answer of a Shinto spirit, but it seemed wise to ask anyway. Perhaps it would guide her feet onto the proper path without her knowing or perhaps it was off bedding a maiden to plant a phantom child. Hitomi smiled at the old story, remembering how many nights as a child she had bound her legs together before sleeping to ensure that she birthed no ghosts.

She bowed once more wishing the *kami* good joy in his conquests and rose to her feet. She dare not rest long, especially not at a crossroads.

Returning the sword to her back, she faced down the trail. Beneath the shining sun, a choice lay before her, one trail to the north, another to the east. They appeared almost identical. Each wide enough to allow two burdened men of the *Ekichiku* clan to pass with their great loads upon their backs. The earth beaten flat by the centuries of feet that had packed the dirt so hard that nothing would ever grow upon the path.

Equally well used, there was no clue telling her which was her path. The smell of the wind only told what she already knew, the clay masters of the great pottery clan lived to the north. To the east, the wind told her—

She dove to the dirt, her instincts and training taking charge of her body long before her mind registered the slight scuff of a bare foot upon hard earth to her back. Even as one shoulder struck the path, the other imparted all of her strength into a throwing star. It caught the bandit in the center of the forehead and split his skull, even as his thrown knife passed above Hitomi's shoulder. Its point drove into the *kami's* right shoulder with a hard thud. She could hear the metallic hum of the blade as it stuck and vibrated.

Rolling to her feet, she batted aside a swung staff barehanded and broke the second bandit's neck.

Neither moved, except to bleed and sink slowly upon the earth as their bodies began to register their deaths. Their scarves of brown cloth were so dirty that they blended with the world around them. Their clothes of the same coarse and plain cloth. Did they wait upon the crossroads for any passerby?

Or did they wait just for her? Was her message compromised?

No sane man would attack a *Mura* and expect to live. But to a pair of bandits, she may have appeared but a *ronin,* a fallen

*samurai* with no clan and no honor. The
*Mura* didn't wear their clan upon their brow
as did so many others. Those who fought,
*Mura, ronin,* or *samurai,* only wore their
headbands to battle or to formal gatherings
with their lord.

She quickly inspected her attackers.
Nothing.

A chill slid up her spine as she watched
the woods around her and patted the men
down. She found no headband tucked
neatly away. Not even a few coins from a
prior robbery. They carried only the swords
upon their backs.

The hard surface of the path bore no
traces to mark the direction of their arrival.

Even a renegade *Mura,* a thought almost
too horrible to contemplate, would have
left more markings on the trail or along the
soft verge into the woods. These two had
shown no sign of the *Mura* weapons or
training. They were much as they appeared,
lordless ruffians, yet they had arrived from
nowhere.

Hitomi knew of no power that could place a man where he had not been a moment before. Even the *Musou* could only place the illusion. These were flesh and blood. She rested a hand over the first as-sailant's stilled heart, his body was definitely solid and still warm.

She pulled the knife that had been planted so deeply in the *kami's* right shoulder that she had to work it free. She imagined that the right shoulder of the wood bled when the point was free. The blade even smelled as if it had it been bathed in the earthy odor of the *kami's* blood.

The right-hand path was the path of blood.

She recovered her throwing star and the knife's sheath from the first dead man, then placed them in her belt. The blade was not a design she knew.

It might be of no importance. The great swordmakers were all known to her, the greatest were the *Mura,* but there were others.

Many clans forged knives for eating and butchering. This one had been forged for killing, but even that was not so unusual. What worried her was that it bore no maker's mark. Nor did their swords.

Hitomi considered burying their swords and the second bandit's knife to keep them from others, but time was short and she merely cast them deep into the woods. The bodies she would leave to the carrion crows.

There was only one conclusion.

A new clan walked the land of the Floating Kingdom.

She wondered if that might be the message locked in her own mind.

One more low bow to the *kami* in thanks, and Hitomi set off at a fast jog along the left path that led her north toward the potters. Now she must cross the land where *raku* was no longer merely a technique to create stoneware for the tea ceremony.

That craft, like her own, had grown over the centuries.

# 3

**Hitomi crossed the land** of the great *raku*
masters in the night, moving with the
darkness as though one with it. Her body
could feel the pull, the need driving at her
heart, gut, and loins.

The mystics of the potters had elevated
their craft to such a height it could reshape
not just one's emotions, but their very
being. Even passing by their kilns ripped at
her soul. But her mental discipline let her
cross through, though she ached with the
battle of it, her mouth bitter with the taste

of blood where she had bit her tongue to provide a focus of pain.

Once north of the great clay pits she traveled easier, and turned north of east toward Edo.

# 4

**One did not simply** walk up to the Son of Heaven in the center of the greatest city the world had ever known. Edo spread for a dozen miles in every direction from the Imperial Palace centered upon Edo Castle. This was a fortress so strong and so layered that even a *Mura* would be unlikely to survive an attempt to enter uninvited.

But that didn't mean she had to plod as others did. The political layers of the court could take months to traverse. Hitomi didn't have the patience, the influence, or the time. Master Tanka could have sent her an introduction direct to the royal chambers, but then she would have been seen. He'd said that no visit by a *Mura* should be noted by the court. She needed another path.

Hitomi brushed by the regions of the city for the serfs and the merchants.

The lesser clans of warriors noticed her passing no more than the wind breathing through the leaves of a forest. She warmed herself at their campfires, ate meals with the bored guards who told stories of the betting rolls of last night's Chō-Han game and their favorite whores working near the geisha district, and passed unremarked by their *diaymos* wrangling for power and presence.

It took her only three weeks to discover her point of entry.

**5**

***Michi Ito, third wife*** to Daiki, the son of the
Emperor, woke slowly to the first hint of
dawn. Her husband had been very active
last night, leaving her sore and spent in the
most pleasant of ways.

She opened her eyes slowly to the
opulent room Daiki had granted her three
months before when accepting her from
her father, the powerful Daimyo Ito. It
had been a canny political move that vastly
elevated her own station. Her rice paper
screens were not painted by the great

masters, but neither were they the work of some lowly apprentice. If one watched the third screen from the left for long enough, the depiction of her garden from home in Ito, the flowers appeared to grow and bloom, but never to fade.

Michi turned for her maid, but caught her breath sharply. Sitting not a foot from her *tatami* mat, a warrior sat in purest black, as if he were a hole cut in the world. Only the eyes gave away that a person actually sat there.

She considered crying for help, but wondered if she would survive to do so and kept her mouth closed.

The shadow offered a slight nod of approval.

"Good. You have common sense." A voice loud enough to be heard, but not to carry beyond her own ears; definitely not to the ears always listening beyond the rice paper in the royal court.

A woman's voice, not a man's. A girl's, perhaps not much older than Michi herself.

She did her best to keep her own voice low though it felt like a black bear's roar beside the woman's simple words.

"I am no fool."

"That is why I have come to you, Chosen Wife."

Was the woman attempting flattery? To have been a chosen wife rather than merely a gift… Michi brushed it aside. To be a gift to the first son of the Son of Heaven was better than being Chosen of some poor maker of court *haiku*.

"I am Hitomi of the *Mura* clan."

Michi felt a chill run up her spine. She had heard of the *Mura*, who had not. But she had never imagined that she would ever meet one. The *Mura* were said to be as forthright as their blades and as deadly.

Swallowing hard, Michi reached deep into her soul for courage and found a small amount sufficient to speak.

"Am I to die?"

The shadow shook her head. "I bear a message for the Son of Heaven, one that cannot wait for…" And she waved a hand toward the walls.

Michi remembered her own presentation at court. Even her own father, the Daimyo Ito, had taken weeks to pass through the court's sycophants so that he might present his daughter as a gift to the Emperor's son.

"And you found me." She made it a statement. There was a logic to it that Michi could appreciate. She had been trained in far more than ways of pleasuring her master, the primary being the dynamics of politics.

This *Mura* would know that Michi could not take her to the Son of Heaven himself. But that her lord Daiki could most certainly place the woman in his father's presence.

Michi rose, unashamed of her nakedness. She knew her body was as near perfection as breeding and conditioning could achieve. Besides, it was a body that belonged to Daiki and it mattered not what this fighter might think.

Michi moved to the basin of water and washed herself. She ignored the fact that it was chill with the night air. Did her maid still live? How was it that she had woken unattended?

She wrapped herself in a simple kimono of the palest blue cotton with adornment only along the hem and belt. Unable to tend her own hair properly, she left it loose to her knees as Daiki liked it.

"Why should I help you?"

"I carry a message, Respected One."

Michi left a silence as she cleaned her teeth.

"I do not know the message," the woman finally spoke. "I only know that it is for none but the Son of Heaven."

"And you have not opened the scroll?"

Michi returned to stand before the woman still kneeling on the hard floor beside Michi's *tatami*. Even awake, with the dawn light now filling the room more strongly, the woman was little more than shadow. She flowed to her feet in a single move more graceful than a Noh performer.

Eye to eye Michi saw three things.

She saw that this Hitomi had been properly named, her eyes were indeed beautiful and it made Michi wonder what she looked like beneath her mask.

Second, Michi saw that the woman truly did not know what message she carried.

Third, Michi saw the embodiment of death more true than all of her father's legions.

**6**

***In the meeting room*** to which she had been
guided by Third Wife Michi, Hitomi knelt
with her forehead upon the *tatami*. In
the small room, she could easily hear the
breathing of the two swordmasters who
stood close behind her. They made no
other noise than the occasional shifting of
their weight from one leg to other causing
the mats to speak softly.

The silence was at long last broken by
the whisper of silk and the brush of slippers
upon the rush straw of the mats. This told

her of four warriors and two courtiers entering. She had thought one of the courtiers might be the Emperor, until she heard his step enter the room. There was no mistaking it.

His tread had neither the lightness of a fighter nor the hesitancy of the courtiers. With a brush of cotton, not silk, he settled to kneel not three steps from her.

"What brings an unannounced *Mura* to see the Son of Heaven?"

"I know not, Heavenly Sovereign. I bear a message. One that will be spoken only if I may look upon your face." Hitomi kept her eyes closed and her forehead upon the *tatami.*

A long silence, a whisper of cotton as the Emperor gestured, and then most of the people left the room. She heard one of the guards behind her leave, but not the other.

"Please sit up, Little Sister."

Taking a deep breath to steel her gut, Hitomi rocked back onto her heels. The simple white room, barely five *tatami* square was empty except for the Son of Heaven and a single warrior directly behind her. He would be the Emperor's best and most trusted.

Then she looked upon the Emperor's face. He was a handsome man, but not a big one. His peasant's kimono of plainest cotton only emphasized that the great ruler's power came from keen insight and his direct heritage from the gods. His hair was graying.

It was enough.

"Master Tanka of the *Mura*," Hitomi felt the memory open and simply allowed the words to flow. "Sends greetings to the Heavenly Sovereign through this most humble of warriors, Hitomi Yamada. She was sent to listen to the conversations of a secret meeting of six southern daimyo at Hiroshima-Jo. She penetrated the castle and discovered a plot against the sanctity of the kingdom. Goro, the daimyo of Hiroshima province itself, wishes to instate himself and his line as the emperor of all lands south of Osaka."

Hitomi now could recall the three long days and nights she had lain in hiding within the Hiroshima Castle. Fear for her life had been trained out of her since birth. She had also learned to master her body's demands, but even the memory left her throat dry and her belly empty, for she had not dared move in all that time.

"Goro has the support of many of the southern daimyo. They meet again on the first day of summer. The *Mura* serve at the Son of Heaven's behest. Please command this Hitomi Yamada and it shall be done."

**7**

***Michi Ito watched Hitomi's*** practice. Hitomi had refused to have others witness what she did, but Michi had indulged herself and refused to leave the girl alone. Finally the *Mura* had relented, allowing her alone to remain.

Michi had procured them a hard-walled room of grey stone and aged wooden beams. Hitomi had inspected the whole of it carefully, perhaps for spyholes. She didn't explain and Michi did not ask. Once through, Hitomi then sat unmoving in the exact center of the room.

Perhaps Hitomi had hoped to bore Michi past tolerance, but she knew the power of waiting as if it were a part of her soul. It was only when—during a single eyeblink—that Hitomi was no longer in the center of the room that Michi understood she was witnessing an art as high as her own.

The *Mura* had stayed still so long, had left such an impression on Michi's mind, that she'd never noticed the warrior depart the room's center. Nor did she see her elsewhere after a quick scan of the room. It was only on blinking hard and looking carefully that she saw the dark eyes watching her from inside her own shadow, the only place the bright afternoon sunlight streaming through the high windows did not reach.

Rather than startling, Michi laughed at the trick, managing due to her training to keep the nerves out of her voice, though they rippled through her stomach.

"You're very steady, Chosen Wife. You would have made a good *Mura.*"

"I was not chosen, I was gifted and accepted." Michi knew no bitterness, but felt the sadness brush across her cheek before she could send it upon its way.

"Five days I waited to see the Son of Heaven and deliver my message. Five more have I awaited an answer. Yet the Emperor's son has come to your bed six of those nights."

"I am the newest. Later he shall weary of me."

"He plays cards with his number one wife and listens most carefully to the castle gossip that she is wise enough to gather for her husband's sake. The Heavenly heir dallies with his number two wife but finds her of no interest beyond the bedroom. He seeks you to challenge himself, both his mind and his body. I can see that your training is as deep as mine, though I do not understand it. You are the Chosen One, it is only that neither of you yet know it."

Michi looked into her own shadow and studied Hitomi's eyes.

"You would have made a good court wife, Hitomi."

The *Mura* laughed. It was the first time Michi had heard it in their ten days together. The third wife on display to a kingdom and the invisible warrior, born but five days apart.

"I think," Michi considered her words, but listened to her heart. "I think we shall be friends."

Hitomi's eyes went wide, then very slowly, never leaving the darkness that was Michi's narrow shadow, she bowed until her forehead touched the hard stone between Michi's feet.

"I should never be so honored."

**8**

**It was hard to** leave. Hitomi had never had a friend who wasn't a warrior. The fighters of the *Mura* clan only spoke of training and battle, strategy and tactic, method and technique.

Chosen Wife had a lively mind that had opened a wider world to Hitomi's consideration.

A world wide enough that when the Emperor commanded her next actions, she took a risk. Hitomi did not simply lock them in her mind as before. The descendant of the many Gods bade her return to the Castle at Hiroshima on a special mission.

They were also the political words of a man fighting to control a Kingdom that stretched across more than two lunar months of walking.

So, Hitomi had not sealed the words away. If she were captured and tortured, they might be revealed. If that occurred she must make sure to die first. Her passage out of the Castle and Edo city were noted only by her new friend.

As she ran south across the span of the Chū-bu and Kansai regions she considered the Emperor's command and the words of his son's third wife.

Perhaps Hitomi's focus was tighter, perhaps she had learned more care. None followed her, none attacked.

Though none helped her either.

She didn't slow, but took without asking what she needed to keep her moving *ri* upon *ri* until she reached Hiroshima.

She did not travel home to Master Tanka.

There was not time for the additional days upon the road. The first of summer was approaching Hiroshima-Jo almost as fast as she did herself.

It was only as she crossed the Otagawa River and entered the castle in the wake of the first-arriving daimyo of Fukuoka, that she understood the Emperor was acting strictly from self-interest, not from heavenly guidance.

Michi had told her that great secret along with a companion truth: all life was politics. Hitomi was unsure what had changed her initial disbelief to present belief, but during her days on the road, it had happened.

It was such a shocking thought that the Son of Heaven was but a master politician, that she faltered and a cook's assistant, noting her for the first time, asked if she belonged here. In answer, she helped an *Ekichiku* burdenman ease his load into the courtyard though he stood several *shaku* taller than Hitomi and his shoulders were so very broad.

The cook shrugged and departed. Hitomi faded back into the shadows before the burdenman could turn and see who to thank.

She had studied the towering central keep of the Hiroshima Castle during her first time here. It rose tier-upon-tier five stories into the sky. The floors were each three times the height of a woman. She followed in the wakes of the shifting patterns of the samurai and worked her way upward. She arrived at the second floor after barely a half day's work and slid beneath a low table. Based on the dust upon its surface, it had not been used since she had last hidden beneath it three months before.

Six hours later, night had fallen and the heat fanned by sake had risen until it roared in the veins of those attending the welcome dinner.

Once above the second story floor, the multi-tiered castle was very easy to traverse. She exited a second-story window onto the roof. At the center of the roof face, a great curving peak sloped upward carrying her to the third floor, then the fourth. The fifth story required only two casts of the grappling hook and she swung into a small room barely twice her height and a half-dozen paces across.

Hitomi studied the room carefully, but little had changed in the three months since she had listened to the daimyos' first meeting upon the night of the vernal equinox.

She moved up into the rafters. They were massive, and few people ever thought to look upward. Fewer still would notice a slender girl lying upon the main center beam as unmoving as the dust and the bones of a long-dead mouse that kept her company.

9

**Six daimyo entered through** the trap door in the floor of the room. Hitomi recognized them all. Each brought a guard, which would be a problem. But after carefully inspecting the room, they departed. Only Goro's guard had thought to inspect the rafters, but his eyes had slid over her shadow without pause.

The six daimyo settled slowly upon their *tatami*.

Hitomi did not try to follow their words, they were the same as before. They were building upon the political base she had learned of at their first meeting. They spoke as if setting the foundation blocks for this second conference. The economic advantages of withholding tribute to Edo, of avoiding the inevitable delays caused by the distant capital.

Goro's predecessor had broken one of the ten thousand rules created by the Imperial Monarchy to control the daimyo. Hiroshima-Jo had been damaged by the spring floods twenty years before. It was against the law to alter one of the Japanese castles without the Emperor's express permission. For two years Sora had awaited permission to fix his castle. Finally, in desperation he had repaired it and made it stronger against the next flood.

The Imperial Court had not answered for a reason, they'd intentionally outwaited Sora's patience.

The trap closed and he was sent to a tiny fiefdom on the northern island of Hokkaido where it was said that summer never came and the rains never left. Goro, a favorite of the court, had been put in Sora's place yet now he proposed seccession from the rule of the Imperial Court.

Hitomi let the words roll over her as she sifted the possibilities through her mind.

The Son of Heaven had left no doubts concerning his own instructions. Hitomi had only moments for a hurried conference with Chosen Wife before she'd left Edo. Michi had convinced her of the importance of doing the task exactly as instructed.

"At least *this* task," she had said. The implications that one might ever disobey the Son of Heaven had shocked her brain awhirl and caused a tightness in her stomach that had not dissipated with the many *ri* she had crossed so quickly.

Hitomi knew nothing of politics, but her instincts told her that her new friend was both wise beyond her years and would never betray their confidences.

As the six daimyo reached the end of summarizing what they had discussed the first meeting, as their tempers rose enough to make them speak loudly over one another despite their unified purpose, that was when she dropped into their center.

She landed squarely upon the closed trap door in the middle of the floor and kicked the bolt home so that none could enter from below.

Even as her feet hit the floor, two of the daimyo clutched their throats where her throwing stars had cut both their windpipes and their vocal cords.

The single, two-handed stroke of her *katana* sword silenced the two who had been whispering together.

Even as their heads tumbled to the floor, Okayama rose to his feet right into the downward driving arc of her sword, cleaving him in two from the top of his head to past his shoulders.

Only Goro did not move.

He did not sit passively, but with an assessing intelligence. He could not have known of her instructions, as she had traveled faster than the fleetest messenger. He had simply assessed the situation and expected an attack.

His expression, and lack of movement were sufficiently surprising that she wondered what she had missed.

Even as she had the thought, she swung her sword up to hold it sideways above her head.

A downward slicing weapon clanged hard against her sword and jarred her arms.

This was the first noise of the battle, and startled cries sounded from below the trap door. Moments later, the first fist pounded upward against the lock.

Hitomi had already spun clear.

She was faced by a single opponent. He was dressed in the same plain brown as the two bandits at the *kami's* shrine along the road to Edo.

She blocked two more blows, startled by his strength and speed. But she was gaining a feel for him. He drove at her, to push her back toward Goro where assuredly a knife awaited her.

Rather than beating back the blow, she dropped her sword to the floor with a clatter that drew their attention down as she leapt for the rafters. Swinging her legs clear, the attacker stumbled forward when his strike found no opposing force.

She dropped back to the floor behind him and drove her shorter Shōtō sword straight through his back and into Daimyo Goro's chest.

Goro studied her, even as the light in his eyes faded. He was not surprised at the warrior who had appeared from thin air. He was surprised that a *Mura* had defeated his secret warrior.

Before she could ask the question, the last of his life's light faded from his eyes.

## 10

***Hitomi Yamada sat before*** Master Tanka of
the *Mura* clan and considered what to tell
and what to keep hidden.

It was a question she was ill prepared to
contemplate. A month before she'd have
no more kept something hidden from her
clan's master than she would have suspected
the Emperor of taking a strictly political
action.

That she had succeeded and returned
unscathed had gladdened the aging master
though he was saddened by the deed.

It had been only the work of moments to learn that the warrior who had attacked her in the highest room of the Hiroshima Castle had no more identification than the two she had left dead by the roadside shrine. It had taken only a few moment's work and Goro's short sword had filled the hole in the warrior's chest where Hitomi had removed her own weapon. She had put the bandit's knife from the attack at the shrine into the warrior's hand and Goro's heart.

Thus Goro would die a hero, defeating his own killer.

The execution of the six daimyo would elevate their sons, or perhaps they too would fall, and the Emperor would set new favorites in their places.

"Life is politics," was the last that Michi had said before sending Hitomi on her way. And Hitomi knew from her own training that until you understood someone's action, to counter the stroke was a fool's gambit.

She knew that warriors existed who could manifest from nowhere.

Hitomi would follow Michi's advice and keep the information about these secret warriors to herself.

It was the *Mura's* task to be the force where mere samurai and soldiers could not prevail.

Now the battlescape of the Floating Kingdom had changed.

And a wiser Hitomi would have to observe—and consider her own next steps very carefully.

# About the Author

*M. L. Buchman* has over 35 novels in print. His military romantic suspense books have been named Barnes & Noble and NPR "Top 5 of the year" and *Booklist* "Top 10 of the Year." In addition to romance, he also writes thrillers, fantasy, and science fiction. In among his career as a corporate project manager he has: rebuilt and single-handed a fifty-foot sailboat, both flown and jumped out of airplanes, designed and built two houses, and bicycled solo around the world. He is now making his living full-time as a writer, living on the Oregon Coast with his beloved wife. He is constantly amazed at what you can do with a degree in Geophysics. You may keep up with his writing at www.mlbuchman.com.

# Nara

**Nara, Japan, February, 2082**

**A *hand descended out* of** the darkness and landed on Ri's shoulder. She knew the hand instantly. Only Tinnai, of the whole cadre, dared touch her without warning.

Others had learned all too well of her hair-trigger reflexes.

"I'm ready, Tinnai." Ri kept her young girl's voice at a barest whisper.

Tinnai's nod was more felt than seen in the darkness. Taking her hand, the cadre leader placed something heavy in it. A pipe. The pipe! Tinnai had been sharpening it for weeks on the concrete. The constant grinding noise now a part of everyone's dreams. The point shone wickedly. Even in the overcast, moonless night, she could see the glimmer of the steel-bright edge. It was almost as long as she was tall. A fearsome weapon.

"Tonight. You guide us." And then, impossibly, Tinnai bowed to her. A shadow upon shadow. Bowed deeply. Honor and respect from the cadre leader. If Ri had still been a young one, she'd have started to cry. But not tonight. Tonight, Tancho Cadre's fate lay in her hands. There had never been a more important fight. And it was hers to lead.

She returned the leader's bow, hefted the pipe to the center of balance, the surface rust rough against her palm, and turned to face along the sidewalk. The cracked concrete beneath her bare feet made her feel more stable. She tried to breathe slowly and shallowly so that the vapor that escaped her mouth into the freezing air would be even less visible in the night.

Tinnai rested her hand on Ri's shoulder. In moments the signal passed up the line just as they'd rehearsed. A squeezed shoulder, from girl to girl up the entire line until Tinnai's hand squeezed Ri's and they were ready to go.

Tonight she didn't run with a small group of hunters. Tonight, the entire cadre hunted the streets of Nara together. Tancho Cadre. The Fighting Cranes. They owned this night. Nineteen girls strong from four to sixteen years old. In the last city of Japan. Maybe the last one on Earth.

She touched the rough brick of the old wall beside her to make sure of her direction and moved forward.

Each crack in the sidewalk an old friend. Walked but twice in a month of planning, once at the beginning to learn, and yesterday to confirm the memory she'd spent four long weeks honing until it sang as a part of her blood.

Fifty-four paces before she reached out again and exactly touched the corner of the brick wall. Her finger traced the small pocket made by a missing chip at exactly the height of her elbow.

She turned right and began a new count. The cadre followed in carefully rehearsed lockstep. The air so cold it had little smell. When it blew from the north, the scent of snow and mountains sometimes clawed into Nara. From the south, it smelled of the sea. From the east was the worst. The smell of cooking, of actual food occasionally rose from Daibutsu-den cadre or from the dark mystery of Nara-ken park. But not tonight. Tonight the air hung still and silent, the wind but another creature holding its breath in the dark.

At fourteen steps, a scuffle by her foot then a squeak as a rat scurried off.

Ri counted to fifty.

All was silent.

She counted to a hundred.

Still nothing.

Fourteen. Her foot had been raised for fifteen. She continued her count and the cadre followed in perfect silence.

At thirty-two she reached out her right hand again and traced the vertical line of the Yen symbol on the steel plaque beside the bank's missing door. She'd asked Tinnai, but no one knew what it meant, only what it was called and that it had been holy.

She turned left and headed across the invisible street toward tonight's target, the one they'd been training to attack for nearly three months. The bookstore lay three and seventeen and two paces ahead.

One. Two. Three. At the curb, she lifted her shoulder high to warn of a change underfoot then stepped off the curb. Weeks of practicing "Follow the Elder" wearing blindfolds paid off. Tinnai's hand shifted as the message passed shoulder to hand down the line of nineteen girls.

Tinnai had berated her for her risks this afternoon. She'd cleared a narrow path through the debris on the street. A little girl, she stood small, even for a ten-year-old, chasing a pretend playmate up and down the street. Hawk Cadre's guards had watched her with disdain. They'd made a fatal mistake and left the silly little girl alone. For once Ri was glad of her small size. In just four heart-stopping passages up and down the street, she'd managed to confirm her practiced distances and to clear tonight's path for the cadre.

She'd had to do it. Rani was clumsy. She couldn't even do the simplest obstacles in the dark without messing up. She didn't cry out after the first hunt she'd ruined. But tonight a stumble, even a scuffed foot, and the whole cadre might go down.

And Tinnai would be far angrier if she knew that Ri had entered the tunnels of the Zenbu beneath the store. A terrible risk, but there she had locked the basement door of the bookstore from the outside, blocking escape. A risk that would cause her nightmares for many nights, if there were more nights.

Seventeen steps, she raised her shoulder and stepped up onto the opposite curb. Only there was no crack in the concrete beneath her bare foot.

Think! Had she veered left or right in the crossing?

She started to slide a foot to the right, searching the surface slick with the night's frost when she heard it. A rattle of teeth.

The sacrificial shivering outside the bolthole. The bookstore's only entry, a knee-high, circular hole. The sacrificial huddled against it for warmth, kept from running away by the chain about his ankle.

She shifted left a half step, felt the concrete crack beneath her foot, took two steps and kicked out. High and hard. Crushing the sacrificial's throat before he could cry out his warning. Leaning in and up at the end of the kick, his neck let go as only a break could cause.

He flopped sideways and Tinnai dove past her into the bolthole. The entire cadre flowed in like a single, long, gutter snake.

Ri ducked through last. By the time she entered, Tancho Cadre flew forward in full motion through the store. The sacrificial's chainkeeper had no more throat to cry with than the one he'd held captive. A knife slash had left only the ability to stare wide-eyed as he bled out. Firelight flickered from the back of the store, the towering bookcases dark silhouettes.

Some of the cadre ran down the aisles. Others had vaulted onto the cases and ran along the tops leaping over gaps at the aisles. At the back of the store, they were only beginning to suspect an attack in full flight. When the ground team met resistance from the Hawks, the high runners fell upon them from above like deadly rain, their long dark hair streaming out behind them.

Ri raced toward the back of the store. Tinnai and Ninka, Tancho's best hunter, were in pitched battle with a pair of boys armed with clubs. Then two more joined in, racing up from what must be the cellar. Stopped by the door Ri had locked against them.

Now they were coming up the stairs behind Tinnai. Perhaps she should have left the door unlocked so that they could escape if they survived the tunnels of the Zenbu. But a free Hawk could seek revenge.

With a cry, "Behind you!" she swung her pipe at the head of one of the attackers. The weight of it carried it so far into his skull she had trouble freeing it. As he collapsed, the man in front of Tinnai also went down. Even as he died, he lacerated her right arm and it dangled suddenly limp.

Her knife dropped and she dove to grab it with her other hand. But her recovery roll was wrong due to her injured arm. Blood was a sharp edge to the scent of night, the smoke from the firepit stung her eyes.

The Hawk Cadre's leader faced Tinnai. He was man-tall, his chin scraggly with a thin growth of whiskers. His companion fully engaged Ninka, she could do nothing to help. With a feral smile, the leader brandished the longest knife Ri had ever seen. Tinnai was in danger.

Ri charged. No cry. Nor stealth. Nor thought. She brushed by Tinnai's elbow and drove the pipe into the leader's chest. The sharpened, shining point punched a hole right into him, only stopped by the bookcase he staggered against.

His knife didn't drop, but he didn't raise it either. In surprise, he looked down to inspect the pipe protruding from his chest. Then he looked at Ri, just as his heart's blood, black in the dim firelight, gushed out the open end of the pipe and sprayed all over her. The heat spread through her clothes and burned against her chilled skin. He toppled silently to the side like a stray leaf on the still winter air.

Tinnai hamstrung Ninka's attacker and a moment later, Ninka finished him off.

The bookstore was silent. No more fighting. No shouts.

Tinnai called roll.

Two didn't answer. Little Rani had killed one Hawk who'd then landed on her and knocked her out against a bookcase. She'd have a good bump for a while, but no worse. Melna was found with a knife between her breasts, but three lay dead around her. An honorable death.

They all turned their attention to the towering bookcases.

Books. Books beyond counting. In the flickering firelight another floor could be seen with more shelves.

"So many books," Ri breathed into the warm night air inside the bookstore. "We have enough heat for a dozen winters!"

*Available at fine retailers everywhere*
*More information at: www.mlbuchman.com*

www.ingramcontent.com/pod-product-compliance
Lightning Source LLC
Chambersburg PA
CBHW050501110726

47899CB00003B/1038